THE NIGHT OF THE TICKLERS

PAUL SHIPTON

Illustrated by Judy Brown

Oxford University Press

OXFORD
UNIVERSITY PRESS

Great Clarendon Street, Oxford OX2 6DP

Oxford University Press is a department of the University of Oxford.
It furthers the University's objective of excellence in research, scholarship,
and education by publishing worldwide in

Oxford   New York

Auckland   Bangkok   Buenos Aires   Cape Town   Chennai
Dar es Salaam   Delhi   Hong Kong   Istanbul   Karachi   Kolkata
Kuala Lumpur   Madrid   Melbourne   Mexico City   Mumbai   Nairobi
São Paulo   Shanghai   Singapore   Taipei   Tokyo   Toronto

with an associated company in Berlin

Oxford is a registered trade mark of Oxford University Press
in the UK and in certain other countries

ISBN 0 19 916921 7   School edition
ISBN 0 19 918522 0   Bookshop edition

Printed in Great Britain by Ebenezer Baylis

Illustrations by Judy Brown

CHAPTER 1

A bad start

The day got off to a bad start. Stoneface Watkins was in the middle of his most boring assembly ever (which is really saying something).

That's when Katy Skinner leaned forward and whispered to me, 'ZZZZZZZZZZZ! Boring! If there was a contest to find the most boring person, old Stoneface would be world champion. Wake me up when it's over!'

3

It wasn't all that funny, but I just couldn't help myself. I burst out laughing. (I always laugh at Katy's rotten jokes.) It came out in a long hiss, like gas coming out of a burst pipe. The more I tried to stop, the harder I laughed. That made Katy laugh too.

And that's when Stoneface Watkins' steel-grey eye fell on us. Of course, 'Stoneface' isn't his real name, but it suits him all right. Our Headteacher is the strictest, most miserable person on the planet. And there's one thing he hates above all other things... kids giggling during assembly.

His voice echoed around the hall like thunder.

'Katy Skinner! Mike Edwards! See me in my office after school!'

That's when I stopped laughing. And *that's* how the day got off to a bad start. I didn't know it then but my troubles hadn't even started yet...

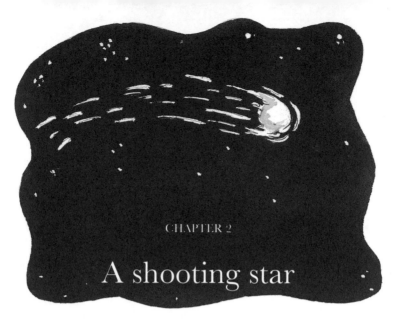

CHAPTER 2

A shooting star

Mr Watkins gave us the same old speech in his office that afternoon.

'You'll have to pull your socks up, I'm afraid, and learn that life is not one big joke. There are some things that you have to take seriously, and school is one of them. School is no laughing matter. And another thing...'

And so on.

We had heard it all before, but that didn't stop Stoneface Watkins from telling us again… and again.

When Katy and I finally left school, it was already dark. Our bikes looked lonely in the bike sheds. They were the last ones there.

Look at the time! My mum'll go crazy if I'm late for dinner.

She unchained her bike and gave me one of her cross looks.

This is all your fault, Mike Edwards! Why did you have to giggle like that in assembly?

MY fault? It was you who made me laugh...

But then Katy shrugged and flashed me her best grin, and I knew I couldn't stay angry with her. I never can. We began to cycle home.

'We can take the short cut by Overton's farm,' said Katy. 'That'll save us a few minutes...'

She turned off onto the jet-black path that snaked up through the woods and over the hill by Overton's farm. I followed. We had cycled halfway up the path when Katy let out a sudden shout.

'Stop!' Her brakes squealed.

I stopped alongside her.

Katy was always trying tricks like that, but I wasn't going to fall for it this time.

She pointed upwards, and I saw a single shooting star zip across the sky over the village of Puddlesford. At first it was just a point of light, like a diamond moving against the blackness.

I tried to sound as scientific as I could.

'"Shooting stars" aren't really stars at all. They're meteors – chunks of rock which zoom through space. They burn up if they enter the earth's atmosphere.'

Well, I've got news for you, professor... This one isn't burning up. It's going to land!

It was true! The point of light was getting bigger. We could see a long tongue of flame behind it now. It was coming closer, and getting brighter and brighter. I tried to tell Katy how unusual this was, but she couldn't hear my voice over the terrible din.

The meteor whooshed overhead and just missed the tops of the trees to our left. Then there was a dreadful crashing sound...

'What was that?' I whispered. My ears were ringing, but I could still hear my heart pounding.

Katy gave an excited grin. 'I don't know... but whatever it was, it just landed.'

CHAPTER 3

Too amazing for Puddlesford

I could hardly believe what I'd just seen.

We'd better go and tell someone. The police or the fire brigade. Anyone!

Of course, Katy had other ideas.

She said, 'Are you nuts? This is the most amazing thing that has ever happened in Puddlesford, and we're going to be the first to see it. Come on!'

She rode off in the direction of the noise. I sighed and began to pedal after her.

Soon the ground was too bumpy to cycle on. We left our bikes and made our way through the trees on foot. I could feel my legs trembling with each step. At first it was totally dark, but soon we began to see a light. There was a faint purple glow ahead of us.

On the other side of the trees, we saw where the light was coming from. It was a huge hole in the ground.

Katy edged closer. I gulped and forced my legs to go on. We reached the edge of the crater and looked over. What we saw made our mouths drop open in surprise.

At the bottom of the hole there was a smooth, silver ball. It didn't look like any meteor I had ever heard of.

My mind raced. Was it...? Could it be...? My head was filled with thoughts of aliens and UFOs from all the science fiction stories I'd read.

The silver ball made a buzzing sound, and a door began to slide open in it. A door! I wanted to run, but I was frozen to the spot.

And then something began to come out of the ball…

CHAPTER 4

Aliens

It was the weirdest creature I'd ever
seen.

In science fiction films there seem
to be two kinds of aliens. Sometimes
they're skinny little aliens with big
heads, who are nice and friendly. And
sometimes they're big, green scaly
aliens who try to eat you, or melt your
brain with a laser blaster.

But this one didn't look like either of those. To be honest, it looked rather funny. (Funny *ha ha*, that is.) Its chubby green body was round as a ball and it had two huge, wide feet. It had a stubby little nose, and a big, lop-sided grin. Its eyes twinkled with mischief.

But oddest of all were the creature's arms. They were long and bendy and each one ended in ten fingers. These fingers were long and slender, but they looked strong.

Katy and I watched in amazement as a second creature came out of the ball. It looked just like the first one. They didn't look scary at all – in fact, they looked friendly, in a goofy kind of way.

Katy cleared her throat. 'Hi there,' she said.

I couldn't believe it! This was probably the first meeting ever between a human being and an alien. Couldn't we think of something better to say than 'hi there'? This meeting would go down in the history books, after all.

The two creatures went on grinning, but they made no sound.

I raised one hand, and put on my best scientist-voice.

Greetings! We... er... the people of Planet Earth welcome you.

'You sound stupid!' hissed Katy. I took no notice.

So... um... where have you come from?

I pointed up at the stars to show that I was asking which planet they had come from. (Of course I knew they hadn't come from the next village!)

The two aliens looked slowly at each other, then they both let out a low sound.

'I beg your pardon?' I said. (I was still trying to be polite.)

The creatures still didn't answer, but something did happen. Something very strange. They began to wave and shake and wobble their arms. As they did this, their arms began to grow longer. Soon their arms were twice as long. Then the aliens began to reach out towards us. Their fingers were waggling.

I still wasn't scared though. The aliens looked so funny and smiley. Maybe they want to shake hands, I thought. I held my right hand out, ready.

But the alien did not take hold of my hand. Instead, it began to waggle its fingers even more.

Hmmm, I thought. Maybe this is how they say hello on their planet?

The two aliens let out their low chuckle again.

Heh, heh, heh

And then it happened...

CHAPTER 5

'Take that!'

The alien began to tickle me.

Ha, ha, ha! Hey stop it! Hee, hee, hee!

The hands were tickling my ribs, its twenty fingers moving faster than the fastest typist. I could hear Katy giggling too. The other alien was tickling her.

I laughed and laughed until tears rolled down my cheeks, and my sides throbbed. I felt like I would explode. But still the alien tickled me. It was horrible! On and on I laughed.

Suddenly I heard Katy shout out.

She smashed down on the alien's
rubbery arms with both her fists. Katy
always was the toughest kid in our
village, and she proved it again now.
The alien's grip was broken. It pulled its
arms back in surprise.

Katy wasted no time. She rushed over and hammered down on the arms of the alien who was tickling me. The creature's grip loosened only for a split-second, but it was long enough. I jumped backwards out of its reach.

For a moment I wasn't sure what to do. The tickling had left me feeling dazed. But then Katy shouted, 'Run!'

So I did.

CHAPTER 6

Heh! heh! heh!

We charged back towards our bikes.
I looked back over my shoulder. The
aliens had climbed to the top of the
crater and were waddling slowly
forwards. They were waving their long,
bendy arms and still making that same
dark chuckle.

It didn't sound
so friendly any
more.

Heh,heh,heh.

For a few endless moments we couldn't find our bikes in the darkness. But then I bashed my shin on one of them.

We scrambled onto our bikes and began to pedal down the path to the village as fast as we could. My sides still ached from being tickled, but I didn't dare slow down.

'Where – where shall we go?' I gasped to Katy.

'Got to get help!' she panted back.

We swerved onto the road that led to the village.

As we raced along, my heart was thudding with fear and excitement. And yet there was a tiny part of me that couldn't help feeling disappointed. I had read lots of exciting science fiction books about aliens invading earth. They were always terrifying monsters that wanted to take over our planet. Proper enemies – not daft-looking creatures that tickled us until we gave up! It was embarrassing.

When we got to the village, the streets were quiet. Too quiet.

I listened.

Aaaa - hahahahahahahaha!

It was the sound of crazy laughter and it was coming from a house on our left. There was a Tickler in there! But they couldn't have beaten us down into the village, could they? It meant only one thing – there were more than two of them. But how many more?

The same sound was coming from the next house, and the next. The village of Puddlesford had already been invaded. We could hear Ticklers in every house! It seemed like the whole village was shaking with helpless laughter. A shiver ran down my spine.

Then someone stumbled out into the street in front of us. We had to swerve to miss him. It was Mr Marshall, the butcher. He was normally a jolly man, but I had never seen him like this before. A Tickler had fixed itself on to the butcher's big tummy, and Mr Marshall was letting out an awful, high-pitched giggle. His face – which was normally red – was now bright purple.

Katy and I jumped off our bikes and rushed to get the Tickler off the butcher. We each grabbed one of its arms and tugged with all our strength. No good!

We began to bash down on its arms, but that didn't work either. Mr Marshall was helpless with laughter. The Tickler chuckled darkly and went on tickling.

Suddenly we heard the noise from behind us.

We spun around. Three more Ticklers were waddling down the street towards us. Another two came out from the shadows.

'Go!' I shouted, but Katy was already back on her bike and pedalling like crazy.

We zoomed down the street, leaving poor Mr Marshall behind us. We were faster than the Ticklers, but I knew we couldn't keep ahead of them forever.

We slowed down when we came to the corner of our road – the road where both our houses were. I could see dark shapes moving at the end of the street. The familiar pavements and front gardens echoed with the new sound of terrible laughter from within the houses.

My mind was filled with a picture of my Mum and Dad being tickled until they were as purple as Mr Marshall, and my brother Joel giggling crazily…

35

Katy shook her head, and I could see how big and afraid her eyes were.

I wasn't so sure. I mean, the Puddlesford police knew what to do if there was a robbery, or if someone parked their car on a double yellow line. But *this*? But I hadn't any other ideas to suggest, so we headed towards the police station on the High Street.

I passed a parked car and two ten-fingered hands made a grab for me. A Tickler! I just managed to dodge out of the way in time.

Katy's voice choked. I looked ahead and saw why. In the darkness we could see a crowd of small round shapes outside the police station. The Ticklers had surrounded it. We could hear the horrible chorus of their chuckles. There was another sound also – the laughter of the policemen and policewomen from inside. We would find no help there.

I glanced behind me. More Ticklers were waddling towards us. Panic seized me in its icy grip. It was clear what we had to do.

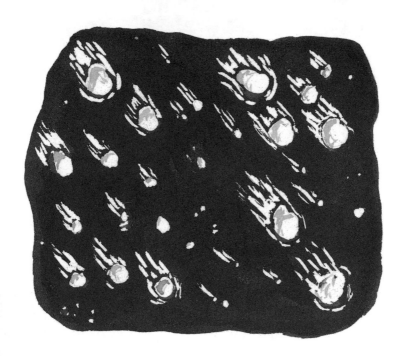

CHAPTER 7

Invasion

We started cycling out of the village.
My legs ached, but I ignored the pain
and forced them to go faster. It felt
good to leave all the sound of laughter
behind us. Now if we could just make it
to the next village and get help...

'Look!' shouted Katy.

A car was parked in the middle of the road. Its lights were on and the driver's door was open. As we got closer we could hear a voice, but when we got there we realized it was coming from the radio. The car was empty.

It was our local radio station. The song began and I was about to click the radio off when the DJ interrupted the music.

This is a news flash. Reports are coming in to the station from people who claim to have seen UFOs – Unidentified Flying Objects. Details are not yet known, but it seems that contact has been made with an alien life form. One eyewitness says that she saw two aliens come out from a silver ball. They then began to tickle people... TICKLE PEOPLE? Is this some kind of joke? It's not April the First, is it?

The DJ did not believe what he was reading. Katy and I just looked at each other. We knew it was no joke.

Suddenly there was a clattering noise on the radio – as if something had been knocked over. It was followed by another sound, one that we knew already: *heh, heh, heh*. A new note of panic appeared in the DJ's voice.

What's going on? Who's there? Wha-
ladies and gentlemen, this is incredible!
An alien has just made its way into the
studio here at Radio Wow FM. I repeat,
there is a creature from another world
here in the studio with me. It's smiling,
it looks friendly. It's moving towards
me now, it's reaching its arms out.
I think it wants to make contact.
I - oo, hey, don't do that! I'm ticklish
- hahaha, no, heeheehee, hooooo -
sssssssssssssssssssss

The radio went dead.

Katy nodded. Her eyes were wide.

We both looked upwards. The dark sky was filled with shooting stars. They lit up the night like fireworks, and we knew that each one carried a load of aliens ready to tickle whoever they met.

'Wha– what are we going to do?'
I said, 'There's no point going to the
next village, they'll be there as well.
It's only a matter of time before they
get us...'

I could hear my voice rising with fear.

But Katy seemed calm again. She was
grinning.

'I've got an idea,' she said. Her eyes
shone. Then she spoke a single word.

Stoneface!

CHAPTER 8

Katy has a plan

There was no time to ask her what she
was talking about. She was pedalling
again, but now she was heading back
towards Puddlesford, back towards the
High Street... back towards the Ticklers.

A Tickler hopped out into our path.
I went to its left, Katy went right.
Luckily the Tickler couldn't make up
its mind which of us to go for.

It waved its arms around trying to decide, and we both rushed past it.

Heh, heh, heh.

It seemed like there were more Ticklers than ever. Another popped out from behind a hedge and made a grab for me. It just caught the edge of my coat, but it didn't get a firm enough grip.

We rode for all we were worth, swerving and dodging and throwing our bikes into almost impossible turns. At last we made it to the other side of the village.

We pedalled the rest of the way in silence. Above us, shooting stars were still criss-crossing the skies.

At last we reached the school. All was quiet. The gates were still open, and a single light was on inside the building. It was Mr Watkins' office – Stoneface often worked late at the school in the evening.

We stood very still and listened. We couldn't hear any sounds of laughter. Slowly we stepped into the school grounds.

CHAPTER 9

Stoneface Watkins

It felt strange creeping through the darkened corridors of our school. I knew it all so well.

There was the artwork on the walls, the chairs stacked up on tables, and the bookshelves in the classroom where I sat every day. They all seemed very important to me now. Maybe you change your mind about things when your planet is invaded by tickling aliens?

As we went on, I could hear
something from further down the
corridor. It wasn't laughter and it wasn't
the chuckle of the Ticklers. It was
someone talking.

Katy had heard it too.

'It's coming from Mr Watkins' office,'
she whispered.

We crept closer to the office. Katy
slowly pushed the door open and we
peeked inside.

Stoneface Watkins was sitting behind his desk, as usual. He was talking to three Ticklers, but they were not like the ones we had seen before. These Ticklers were slumped against the wall. Their arms hung lifelessly by their sides. Their eyes were glassy, as if they were half-asleep.

'And another thing... I think it is extremely bad manners to arrive here without telling us first. It's no excuse to say that you come from another planet – good manners are important anywhere. And as for going around tickling people! Well, it just isn't on, is it? You'll have to pull your socks up if you want to get ahead on Planet Earth. And another thing...'

Stoneface Watkins went on and on. It was clear what had happened. The Ticklers had attacked, but they had been unable to make the Headteacher laugh. (This wasn't surprising – *nothing* made our Head laugh.) So Stoneface had started to tell them off, and it had sent them all into a kind of sleep-state.

Katy beamed at me.

I knew they'd never get him. Not Stoneface – he's our secret weapon!

I was still worried. I knew it wasn't over yet, not by a long way.

What about all the other Ticklers?

But Katy had thought of this too.

'We'll go with Mr Watkins in his car to the local radio station,' she said. 'We'll break through the Ticklers if we have to. With Stoneface to help us we'll be okay. Then we'll broadcast his voice right across the area. That should do the trick! It'll send them all off to sleep.'

I grinned at Katy.

You're a genius, Katy Skinner!

And that's when it happened. Stoneface Watkins did not stop talking for a moment, but he looked up at us, gave us a little smile... and then he winked at us. Winked! Stoneface Watkins! Sometimes, out of all the amazing things that happened that day, I think that wink was the most amazing thing of all!

CHAPTER 10

The universe is a big place

The plan worked.

Of course it made it into all the newspapers:

Daily Telegram

Headteacher defeats aliens

Gregory Watkins, Headteacher of Puddlesford Junior School, was hailed as a hero yesterday, when he helped put an end to an alien invasion. The alien creatures, known to some as 'Ticklers', had invaded a small area of the country, but it is thought that this was just the beginning of their plans.

Mr Watkins' voice was broadcast from local radio station Radio Wow FM, and it sent many of the aliens into a sleep-like trance, allowing many people to escape.

When questioned by our reporter, Mr Watkins said that he had simply treated the invaders in the same way as he would treat his own pupils.

MR GREGGRY WATKINS

Daily Moon

On yer bikes, Ticklers!

The invading army of alien Ticklers got back into their little silver ships yesterday and went back to wherever they come from. An eyewitness who saw one of the ships leave said: 'The creatures seemed keen to go, and they weren't laughing much when they went.'

Inside today's Magic Moon: Ten things you didn't know about those terrible Ticklers – see page 2!

It seemed like every TV programme for a month was about the Ticklers. Of course, nobody could talk about anything else for a while. It isn't every day that aliens try to invade Earth, is it?

But in the end, things went back to normal.

School is the same as ever – Mr Watkins' assemblies are still pretty boring, but I don't giggle during them any more. Whenever I feel like giggling, I just remember the way he winked at us that time in his office.

As for me and Katy… we didn't go near Overton's farm for ages. But then one night it just seemed like the right time. We rode up the path near where the Ticklers had landed.

We stopped our bikes at the top of the hill and looked up at the sky. It was a clear night, and we could see lots of stars. I knew Katy was thinking about that night – the night of the Ticklers.

But Katy shook her head uncertainly. She's more serious now than she used to be.

'The universe is a big place, Mike,' she said. 'It must be full of many different life-forms. And now they know that we're here on Earth. And they know we're ticklish...'

About the author

When I was growing up
in Manchester, I always
wanted to be an astronaut,
a footballer, or (if those
didn't work out for any
reason) perhaps a rock
star. So it came as
something of a shock
when I became first a
teacher and then an editor
of educational books.

I have lived in Cambridge, Aylesbury, Oxford
and Istanbul. I'm still on the run and now live
in Chicago with my wife and family. Like Mike
in the story, I have read lots of books about
alien invasions, so if one ever happens, I think
I'm ready!

Other Treetops books at this level include:

Danny's Secret Fox by Susan Gates
Petey by Paul Shipton
Climbing in the Dark by Nick Warburton
Okay, Spanner, You Win! by David Clayton
Grace the Pirate by James Riordan

Also available in packs
Stage 14 pack B   0 19 916926 8
Stage 14 class pack B   0 19 916927 6